To: Korbin
From: Barbara and Char
December, 2017

For Lila and Emma,
in loving memory of Ben Who Climbs Mountains xxx
S.P-H.

For Theodore xx
E.E.

Sandy Creek
NEW YORK

An Imprint of Sterling Publishing
1166 Avenue of The Americas
New York, NY, 10036

Text © 2016 by Smriti Prasadam-Halls
Illustrations © 2016 by Ed Eaves

ISBN 978-1-4351-6517-5

Manufactured in China
Lot #:

2 4 6 8 10 9 7 5 3 1
10/16

www.sterlingpublishing.com

Ready, Set, RESCUE!

Smriti Prasadam-Halls   **Ed Eaves**

We are **EMERGENCY CONTROL,**
To save and rescue is our goal.
Responding **FAST** to every call,
To every crisis, big or small.

For any rescue we're prepared.
We're very brave. We're never scared.
We'll always be there, come what may,
Ready, set...

ON OUR WAY!

A **FIRE** at the baker's shop!
They need our help to make it stop!

FIRE TRUCK FLICK has got her hose.
Sound the siren! Off she goes!

Flames are **FIZZING,** water **WHIZZING,**

TOW TRUCK TOM'S
the one they need.
Here he comes
to take the lead.

GRIPPING tight, with all his might,

Safely harnessed, nice and slow,
Ready, set... *TOW, TOW, TOW!*

LIFEBOAT LEELA launches fast,
Skims the water, speeding past.

Lightning **FLASHING**,

thunder **CRASHING**,

Hurry, hurry, **POLICE CAR PETE,**
The thieves are zooming
down the street!

ROARING, RACING,

AMBULANCE AL has soothing gel,
And medicine to make her well.

DASHING, DARING, careful, caring,

HELICOPTER HARMIT'S here,
Blades a-whirring,
have no fear.

SEARCHING,
FINDING,
winch **UNWINDING,**

Strong and stable,
firm and swift,
Ready, set... **LIFT, LIFT, LIFT, LIFT!**

There's SO much work we have to do...
We'll need the help of **ALL THE CREW!**

Stop the traffic,
please make way,

Ready, set...

SAVE THE DAY!

The smoke is thick. The work is tough,
But we are big and strong enough.

HEAVING, STRETCHING,

PULLING,

FETCHING,

Help and rescue, lift and tow,

READY, SET...

What a busy day
it's been.
What a lot of things
we've seen.

Climbers rescued,
bad guys caught,

Patients patched up,
fires fought.

Sturdy, steady, **EVER** ready,
Rescue team, we **SAVED** the day...

HOORAY!